UNSEEN RAINBOWS,
SILENT SONGS

THE WORLD BEYOND HUMAN SENSES

by **Susan E. Goodman**

illustrated by
Beverly Duncan

UNSEEN
RAINBOWS,
SILENT SONGS
THE WORLD BEYOND HUMAN SENSES

ACKNOWLEDGMENTS

I would like to thank the following experts for their help: Don Wilson (bats) and Addison Wynn (snakes) at the Smithsonian Institution, Herbert Levi (spiders and bees) at Harvard University, Jelle Atema (catfish) at Boston University's Marine Program, Jerry Rovner (wolf spiders) at Ohio University, Mike Horn (time) at Stonehill College, Bob Wilson (birds) at Boston's Franklin Park Zoo, and Randy Morgan (insects) at the Cincinnati Zoo. A special thanks to ethologist Donald Griffin at Harvard University's Concord Field Station for reviewing the entire manuscript.

For other help along the way, thanks to Deborah Hirschland, Zach Klein, Jeff Goodman, Marjorie Waters, Nancy Powell, Donna DeVaughn, Joyce Mallory, Maxine Rosenberg, Debbie Jose, and Stephen Krensky.

A special thanks to Marcia Marshall, whose kind, easygoing expertise helped transform my manuscript into this book.

SRA Part No. R19983.25

Printed by SRA/McGraw-Hill.
This edition is reprinted by arrangement with Atheneum Books For Young Readers,
Simon & Schuster Children's Publishing Division.
Text copyright © 1995 by Susan E. Goodman,
illustrations copyright © 1995 by Beverley Duncan. All rights reserved.

The text of this book is set in Horley Old Style Bold
The illustrations are rendered in watercolor

First edition
Printed in Mexico
10 9 8 7 6 5

Library of Congress Cataloging-in-Publication Data
Goodman, Susan E., date.
Unseen rainbows, silent songs : the world beyond your senses / by Susan E. Goodman : illustrated by Beverly Duncan.
1st ed.

1. Senses and sensation—Juvenile literature. 2. Physiology, Comparative—Juvenile literature. [1. Senses and sensation. 2. Animals Physiology.] I. Duncan, Beverly, date, ill. II. Title.   QP434.G65 1995   591.1'88   94-10209
SUMMARY: The senses of animals are described and compared to those of a human boy on a summer evening.

To "my greatest fan," Deborah Hirschland, who believed in this book—and, in me
—S. E. G.

For my mother and father, with love
—B. D.

Finally, you're at the cottage! Leaving your family to unload the car, you run ahead, then tumble onto the ground to enjoy the end of the country day. A piece of clover tickles your cheek. Its sweet smell teases your nose. Your dog flops down to pant in your ear as you open your eyes to the blue of the sky and watch an igloo-shaped cloud float past.

After your noisy car ride, the country seems so quiet and peaceful. For you, perhaps, it is. But this same country twilight is also home to another world. A world that dances and sings, lives and dies, beyond the reach of your senses.

OWL EARS AND BAT VOICES

A rabbit stirs far, far down the road. You don't hear anything, but your dog jumps to her feet. She can gather any sound much better than you can. People's ears are small and flat against their heads. We have nine muscles that are supposed to move them. You may know a few people who can use some of these muscles to wiggle their ears. But for most of us, these muscles don't work.

That dog next to you has seventeen such muscles that work just fine. She can prick up her ears, making them taller and wider, to better catch the sound of the rabbit's paws brushing against some dry twigs. She can swing her ears around to bring that sound in even louder.

You hear the dog whimper and watch her dash away. Then you go back to watching the clouds with no clue a rabbit is racing for his life.

Not far away, a little field mouse quietly rustles through fallen leaves. You hear the noise faintly, but you'd have a hard time finding her in the twilight and its dark shadows. An owl could. In the blackest night—never seeing the mouse, never smelling her—an owl could swoop down at top speed and grab her in his talons. The owl is so good at locating sound that you could say he sees with his ears.

Having ears on both sides of your head helps you know where a sound is coming from. You know when a bell's ring comes from your left because you hear it sooner in your left ear—and louder too. An owl uses the same system to find the direction of a sound. But he can also pinpoint its height because one of his earholes is higher than the other.

Knowing where a sound comes from, left or right, up or down, lets the owl zero in on his target. It's as if he could draw a sound map, putting a great big X exactly where the mouse is standing. With the crackle of just a few leaves, an owl can find a mouse as easily as you could spot a lit flashlight.

Noises make the air shake. These vibrations travel through the air in waves. Each minute, millions of these sound waves wash up against your ears, where some of them change into the noises of your world.

Here in the twilight, these sound waves play a country concert. You can hear crickets drumming out the beat of summer's song. Birds—robins and finches, thrushes and wrens—sing the chorus. A passing plane adds a growl to the music, while mosquitoes whine close to your ear.

Your ears seem filled with the sounds you can hear, but many others pass you by. Creatures are calling to their families, screaming of danger, singing the songs of their lives in voices you cannot hear. They are listening to the movements of their next meal, to invitations and warnings, reacting to noises you cannot take in.

Imagine the world of sound as a piano that has thousands and thousands of keys. Like most people, you can sing and hear many of the middle notes, but none above or below them. You hear only part of a tractor trailer's rumble. The rest is too low for you to hear. When the driver stops suddenly, you only hear some of the brake's screech. The rest is high above your range of hearing.

Have you ever heard the cry of a mouse trapped between a cat's two front paws? It's a horrible sound, but only part of that mouse's fear. Like the squeal of brakes, a mouse's squeal combines notes you can hear with terror high above your hearing.

Mice also call out to warn one another of danger. But the sounds are so high they become a secret language. We can't hear them. Luckily for mice, neither can cats.

As your eyes drift from the clouds to the trees, a flash of brown darts by

so fast that you wonder if you saw it at all. It is a bat, swooping through the country twilight, using sounds high above your hearing. When this bat makes his cry, he is talking to every part of the world around him. And the world answers him with echoes.

The bat's sounds travel through the air until they bump up against something and bounce back in his direction. He hears your echo, the dog's, the echo of one tree branch, then another. He uses these sounds to create a picture of his world. Using higher and lower notes, faster and slower sounds, the bat draws a picture so complete that, in the darkest night, he can detect a wire no thicker than a strand of your hair.

You probably wouldn't see that wire, even in daylight. In some ways, the bat sees better with his ears than you do with your eyes. If your hearing were as good, you'd be able to pick out a friend's whisper deep within a noisy crowd at a football game.

YOUR country evening is peaceful. Yet, while you dreamily scratch the dog's belly, bats and moths are fighting deadly battles in the sky right above you. The bats begin by sending out high cries and listening for the echoing answer of food. Most insects have no way to hide from the bats' patrol, but some moths have a secret defense. They can hear a bat's call before the bat can

hear their echo. At this instant, moths, like the spinner or looper moths, just stop flying. Wings folded, they plummet downward, hoping to reach the ground before the bat finds their echo and begins his deadly swoop.

Arctiid moths have a more daring battle plan: They fly straight toward danger. Only inches away from the bat, they screech high-pitched cries of their own. Sound waves crash into sound waves, and the moths try to dash away during the confusion.

While you listen to a few crickets in your peaceful night, this battle's rat-a-tat-tat screams as loudly as machine-gun fire. It is a good thing bats' cries use notes high above your range of hearing. They are as loud as jackhammers and would hurt your ears. Imagine the sound of your country night as two, ten, twenty bats streak the sky in search of food.

HEAT MAGNETS
AND STILL BREEZES

Without even moving a muscle, you are busy touching. The sore on your knee feels your pants pressing down on it. A light tickle tells you an ant is climbing your shoulder.

Touch makes things real. It brings the world right up to your own body. Touch also tells you a lot about what is going on around you. It can prove that what your eyes see is true. Yes, the cat's coat is as soft as it looks. That stone is sharp.

Touch can also replace your eyes. When you wade into the nearby pond, your feet use touch to pick their way through slimy plants and rotting leaves to the sandy bottom.

Touch lets you feel very hot things from a safe distance: a roaring fire from several yards, a lit stove burner from a few feet away. You have a much harder time, however, feeling the heat from your television set. And parents must actually touch children's foreheads to see if they have a fever.

To the female mosquito buzzing toward you, your body, sick or well, burns like a fiery magnet, even from yards and yards away. The mosquito knows to turn toward the warmth. When each of her antennae senses exactly the same temperature, she is heading in your direction. Using your heat upon her antennae as her compass, she flies toward you and that sip of blood she needs to lay her eggs.

17

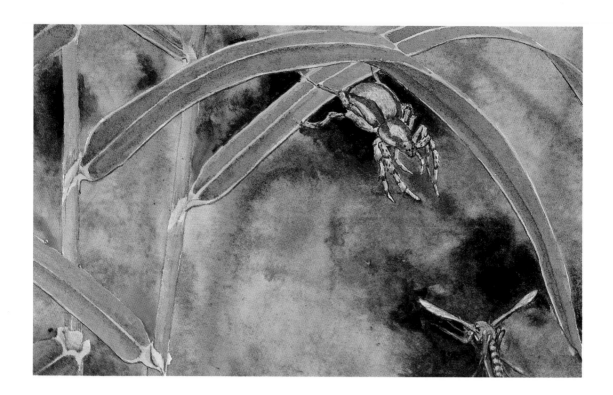

You can tell which way a strong breeze is blowing by its feel against your skin. Yet, the breeze sometimes whispers so faintly your skin cannot help you guess the wind's direction. Even if you look to the trees for a clue, their nodding leaves can't give you the answer.

There, balanced upon some grass just a few feet away, a wolf spider can feel the direction of wind so soft it doesn't move the leaves at all. He does this by using the long, thin hairs on his legs. Like instruments in an orchestra waiting for their signal from the conductor, each hair plays only when touched by air coming from a single direction. The breeze sets off first one hair, then another, and then another, until their movement, played together, tells the spider exactly where the wind is coming from.

But this wolf spider doesn't care about country breezes. He has been waiting, perhaps hours, for that softest stir created by a mosquito's wings. And now that he has found one, he aims himself perfectly to leap and capture his meal.

Imagine a world forever in twilight except when swallowed by the black of night. This is the world of your country pond, where sight and smell are not always enough to provide safety. Luckily, fish have an extra sense to protect them. Dots, running down the sides of their bodies, feel movements in the water and let the fish know what lies around them. These dots, called the lateral line system, give fish a long-distance sense of touch.

When water flows around a big rock, it pushes against the fish in a way that tells them where the rock is and when to turn. Fish in schools can feel when they are safely surrounded by friends. A whoosh in the water pushes against their dots to warn them a hunter fish is near. Some male fish even fight by swimming alongside each other, then wildly flapping their tails. They are *yelling* at each other's lateral line systems about who should rule that corner of the pond.

When night is at its very darkest, you would barely see black upon black if you moved your hand against the sky. In this gloom, some of the best animal hunters might miss their prey. Yet the rattlesnake, gliding through a country night, will slither toward his mouse dinner as surely as he would in the light of day. Rattlesnakes, like all other members of the snake family called pit vipers, have an extra set of "eyes" that see only heat.

The snake's picture of his prey is painted by the mouse's body temperature. The mouse hides beneath some fallen leaves, standing as still as her fear will let her. But it is hopeless. Her heart beats, beats, beats, pushing her temperature warmer than the summer night around her. Her frightened, furry body glows, a target's bull's-eye, for when the snake decides to strike.

MOTH PERFUME AND SWIMMING TONGUES

Suddenly your stomach answers the birds and crickets with a song of its own. You're hungry. Luckily, you have some mint Life Savers in your pocket. If you were a dog, you'd have smelled them in your pocket. If you were a fish, you'd have tasted them in your pocket. But you're a human, so you remember that you saved a few for a moment just like this one. As you take a piece, your sense of smell paints pictures of red-and-white candy canes.

Your sense of smell does more than just pick out this minty perfume. To taste the candy, you need both your nose and your tongue, your senses of smell and taste. Your tongue gives you the basics. It tells you about the candy's sweetness, the saltiness of pretzels, the sour in pickles, the bitterness of orange peel.

But, unless your nose pitched in with a food's smell, you would never taste its full flavor. Your mint candy would be a hard stone in your mouth until it melted and disappeared. An apple would keep its crunch, but it wouldn't taste much different from a chunk of raw potato.

One big difference between your senses of smell and taste is that you can smell foods far away from you. You can only taste them, however, once they've passed over the little bumps on your tongue called taste buds.

Life is different for the bullhead catfish that hovers in the darkness of your country pond. He does use his sense of smell to find the fleshy scraps left over from another fish's dinner. But he has also tasted them long before he swims near. The catfish has so many taste buds, all over his body, that he is like a swimming tongue.

The taste of food brushes up against a catfish the same way a breeze rustles the hairs on your arm. It might be better to say these tastes of food gust up against the catfish like strong winds. You see, the catfish can taste so much more than you can. He finds the tang of plants, snails, fish in what tastes to you like plain pond water. And if you shared a piece of trout, the catfish would taste flavor after flavor that you will never know.

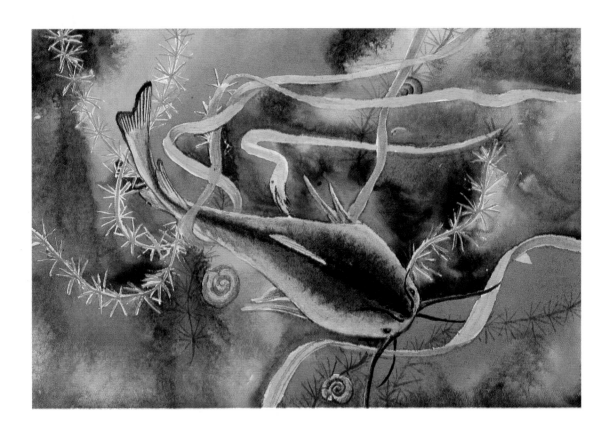

If you called out softly, someone near your car would answer. If you yelled louder, you could be heard even far across the country road. Moths, with a language that uses scent instead of words, can send messages out over miles.

When a female moth wants a partner, she sends the tiniest dab of perfume into the air. The wind picks up her announcement, blowing it, spreading it this way and that. You could never smell it. But if the breeze brings just the smallest hint of invitation to a male moth's antennae, his wings begin to vibrate. He soars up to face the scent and battle the wind, flying to find his mate.

How many different smells are there in your world? You can begin the list with those in a country night: the scent of sweet clover, of crushed pine needles, of the mosquito repellent on your arms. Then you can add the smell of bubble gum, baking cookies, cap guns, sidewalks after a summer rain. Maybe you can come up with a hundred, even two hundred odors. Yet scientists believe we can smell about twenty thousand different scents.

Twenty thousand different odors may seem like a lot, but they are just the beginning of what a dog can smell. For dogs, each and every being—each person, cat, bird, porcupine, even turtle—has a perfume all its own.

Your dog can not only distinguish between odors better than you, she can just plain smell them better too. In fact, to explore the country, you use your other senses more than your sense of smell. Your eyes define your world, telling you where you are. Then they team up with

your ears to tell you who and what is around you.

But a dog's senses are different, so they create a different world. The dog beside you sees a gray world of blurry shapes and shadows. What makes it clear is sound, and wave after wave of smell. When she comes up to give you a sniff, she can smell you and your friend who borrowed your jacket the day before. She can even smell the spot where yesterday's hot dog brushed against your pants on its way to the floor.

Deep behind the bridge of your nose, you have a patch of cells the size of a small postage stamp that lets you smell the world. The dog beside you has a patch the size of fifty postage stamps. Her nose smells a million times better than yours. If the odor you could smell in an average-size room were spread out evenly, it could be detected by this dog in a room two and a half miles wide and two and a half miles long.

EAGLE EYES AND A
HONEYBEE'S RAINBOW

A honeybee buzzes close to your cheek as she flies toward a hawthorn tree's white blossoms. At least, you say the hawthorn's blossoms are white.

A bee's eye works with a different paint box of colors than yours. Bees cannot see red. But they do see ultraviolet, a color we cannot see. This ultraviolet tints many flowers and leaves, mixing with blues and greens to paint a very different world.

If you looked through the bee's eyes, those hawthorn blossoms would be bluish green. And the tree's green leaves would be a dull gray background, making the flowers shine even more brightly. The red berries on a nearby bush would be black. Each daisy petal would have a colored tip so it would look like someone drew a circle around the flower's outer rim.

Other flowers, plain to you, have stripes dancing from edge to center. You can't see them but, then again, you don't need to. The bee spots these *honeyguides* and uses them first as runways to land, then as road signs to the flower's nectar.

Your eyes see three basic hues—red, green, and blue—that split and combine to make all the colors of your rainbow. The fruit fly crawling on an old apple core can only see three different shades of color. You can see millions. Just look around your country night. The leaves on the trees aren't just green, but emerald and jade, pea and olive. The sunset glows with countless pinks and purples. As the light fades, the bush's red berries deepen, turning even redder before they pass into the grays of twilight.

Even in this fading light, you have no problem spotting someone in the pond. Your eyes pinpoint exactly where he is standing. They focus on his face, letting you know he is smiling and friendly. They follow him as he walks away. You are used to seeing the world clearly and completely, but few other animals have eyes that can do all these things.

Since you see so much, it is hard to imagine there are things you cannot see well—and things you cannot see at all.

Far above you, for instance, you can barely see the huge hawk riding the roller-coaster winds of the upper sky. The bird is so high, you can't know if she is black or brown, or even if she has a small bird in her talons. As you look up, however, she can tell the color of your eyes.

Up close, you can see detail after detail. Examine your hand and you see lines traveling everywhere, a dot of dirt under one nail, a tiny freckle near your thumb. Look into the distance and your world fades into outlines, shapes, and blobs of color.

The hawk can see clear details from eight to ten times farther than you can. Imagine standing with the hawk on your shoulder, both of you looking at the same hawthorn tree across the field.

You see a shaggy tree with some branches growing outward, others drooping toward the ground. You see green mixed with some white; real shapes are clear only at a branch's tip, where leaves and blossoms are outlined against the sky. Peeking through the green curtain, you see the dark of inside limbs.

But the hawk sees an ant crawling on a dark glossy leaf. She sees a fly landing on another leaf spotted by spring frost. She sees the green tips of branches edge into brown where they thicken into sturdier wood. Most important, to the hawk at least, she sees deep into the leaves to the inner branches, where smaller birds are nesting their young.

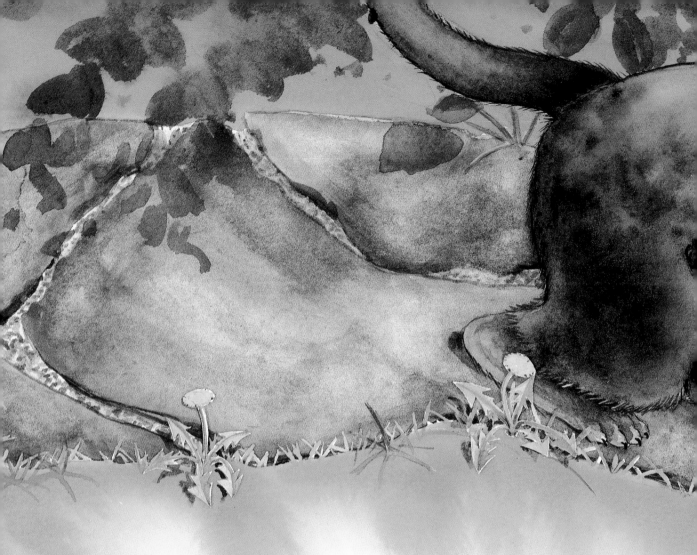

You have the kind of eyes that help an animal hunt and kill. You have predator's eyes, which can look forward and work together to measure how near or far things are from you. This same ability to judge distance helps another predator, the cat, spot a mouse and decide where she must pounce to make her kill.

The mouse's survival depends on seeing that cat slink up from behind or seeing an owl swooping down from the sky. Like rabbits, deer, and many other prey animals, the mouse has eyes on both sides of his head. Each eye patrols its side of the world—front, back, up, down—for a hint of danger. A mouse's eyes don't need to work together to tell him something is five or eight feet away. Their job is to pick up movement coming from any direction. The mouse's eyes send the message, "Something's coming, better run!"

The cat's eyes tell it, "There it is; go get it!"

LIFE IN SLOW MOTION
AND OVERDRIVE

You gaze at the trees waving in the wind but, after a while, you aren't really seeing them. Your thoughts are off, secretly dancing on the same breeze.

Later, you can't remember what you've been thinking about—or, for how long. During this period you have been outside time.

Your sense of time teams up with the rest of your senses to define your world. It helps you wake up early for a favorite television show. Unfortunately, it isn't always as accurate at six in the evening, to get you home in time for dinner. We humans aren't so good at estimating time while we are awake. That's why we invented watches.

That bee, flying through the country twilight, is a living timepiece. She will show up one place at 10:00 A.M., another place at noon, day after day.

Even if you took away the changing temperature and light that help mark night and day, she could keep her precise schedule. If you could gauge time like this, you'd never be late for meals. You'd be just like the bee, who buzzes up to daisies and clover in early morning, the time when these flowers are most full of nectar.

But early morning is long over; in fact, the sun is disappearing from your country night. You share this sunset and the next sunrise, the rhythms of night and day, with the life around you. But how you experience this time span depends on who and what you are.

Like smell, taste, touch, sight, and hearing, time is different for different living things. Your sense of time is unlike that of the mayfly, who passes from an insect's childhood through old age in just a few months. Time would also be different for an imaginary creature whose life stretched over thousands of years. Your life until now—your years as a baby, the days in school, the hours eating, sleeping, playing—would be but a few moments to such a creature.

That fly buzzing around you only has three weeks to live. Don't feel too bad for him, though. His senses work so much faster than yours that he lives at a much faster pace than you.

Just try catching him. The fly sees and reacts at such high speed, your falling hand looks no faster than a slow-motion movie. He sees each beat of a dragonfly's wings where you can see only a blur. A regular living room lamp flickers on and off for the fly. But for you the lamp flickers so fast you see only a steady light.

If this fly wandered into a movie theater, he'd never see that spaceship zooming into warp speed. You do because twenty-four photographs rush by each second—fast enough to create the exciting blur of action the way a flip book turns separate drawings into a moving cartoon. To the fly, however, the movie is just one still picture. Then another. Then another.

Near the pond, a snail inches along, looking for its algae dinner. Time—and life—move very slowly for a snail.

When you take a stick and tap it once lightly on its head, the snail oozes into its shell for safety. But if you tap-tap-tap-tap, four times in less than one second, it tries to crawl onto the same stick it avoided before. The stick feels as if it's pressing on the snail's head so the snail thinks it has crawled into a wall.

If someone tapped your head at this rate, you'd feel each and every tap. But if they tapped fast enough, about eighteen times each second, you'd feel these taps as a steady pressure. That is what happens to your snail. It experiences anything moving faster than four times a second as not moving at all.

In the country twilight, or wherever you are, your senses are your window onto the world. So it is easy to think that whatever you see, hear, smell, taste, and touch *is* the world. But it is, after all, only your world. To say nothing lies beyond what you know is like saying something disappears when you close your eyes and can no longer see it.

No animal has senses that capture everything happening around it. You see white when flowers dance with color. The rattlesnake who sees heat pictures can barely hear. You know only silence in the midst of another animal's music. Pigeons, who can pick up sounds so low they hear the deserts hum, have a very poor sense of smell. You, too, smell nothing when other animals are dizzy with the promise of food. But the dog who can smell far across a field can only see in black and white.

Luckily, you don't have to nose out your dinner. It is ready and waiting for you. You get up and slowly start back. In the ever-darkening twilight, your eyes can no longer find the wolf spider or the mosquito. Even the bat and his battles are hidden behind the screen of night. But you can still see what you need to see—the gray outline of the cottage, with the people you love right on its porch.

Every animal—including you—senses part of the world. All of us have ways to understand how to find food, to react to danger, to find safety. Every type of animal has the package of senses it needs to live its special life. Unless things are very close, cats see in shades of gray instead of color. But these night-time hunters don't need a world painted in brilliant reds and greens. Instead, their eyes take in and use the dimmest light eight times better than ours. What could be more important to an animal who stalks the night for food?

Actually, your package has something extra thrown in—and that is imagination. Your imagination can take you to visit the worlds your senses cannot reach. You can use it here in the country night. Or you can save it to study the countryside as you soar with a hawk in those magic moments at bedtime, just before sleep.